Jeremy and the Ghost

Jeremy and the Ghost

by Elizabeth Charlton

illustrated by Celia Reisman

DANDELION BOOKS
Published by Dandelion Press, Inc.

His whole name was Jeremy David Porter, but no one called him that. No one even called him Jeremy except his mother and father and a few other grown-ups. All the kids on Walnut Street called him Fraidy-Cat.

Jeremy didn't like it a bit. He wasn't afraid of so many things. Just the attic in his grandmother's house. And big, barky dogs. And going to sleep with the hall light off. And mean Marvin McGraw, who lived next door. And most of all, the haunted house on the corner.

Jeremy always crossed the street when he passed the haunted house. It was big and dark and creaky, and it felt empty when you passed by. And Jeremy knew that a terrible ghost lived there. Jeremy's father said there were no such things as ghosts. But Jeremy knew. The house was haunted.

On the day before Halloween, Jeremy remembered that he needed a costume to wear to school the next day. He was tired of being a pirate. He was too big for his Indian suit. And his mother said he absolutely couldn't be a tramp.

Jeremy went upstairs and looked in his father's closet. But everything there was much too big. When he tried on his father's fishing hat, it flopped way down over his eyes.

He looked in his mother's closet, but there were mostly dresses there. He could just hear Marvin McGraw laugh if he came to school dressed like a lady.

Then Jeremy had an idea. In the linen closet were some old sheets that his mother used for dustcloths. He got one out and cut two holes in it for eyes, and one for a mouth. Then he got his paint set. He made two big orange circles around the eye holes. He made a mean, nasty, purple mouth with crooked teeth.

He put on the sheet and looked in the mirror. He looked pretty scary.

Jeremy went to his bottom drawer, where he kept a lot of useful things. He found two pieces of wire all curled up at the ends, and attached them to the top of the sheet. He found a paper cup and painted it green and pinned it where the nose should be. Then he put on the sheet and looked in the mirror again. He looked *very* scary.

"Boo!" he said to the mirror.

Jeremy went downstairs to the kitchen, where his mother was making dinner.

"Boo!" said Jeremy, and she dropped the salad in the sink.

"My goodness," she said. "You frightened me."

Jeremy went to the playroom, where his sister Mary Anne was painting a picture.

"Boo!" said Jeremy, and Mary Anne ran behind a chair. Then she poked her head out.

"Oh, it's only old Fraidy-Cat," she said.

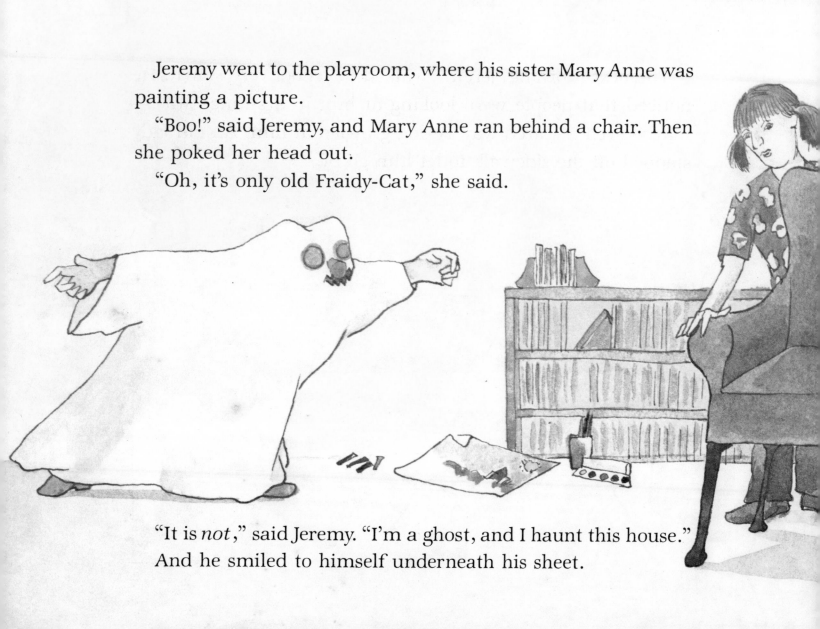

"It is *not*," said Jeremy. "I'm a ghost, and I haunt this house." And he smiled to himself underneath his sheet.

The next morning, Jeremy walked to school very slowly. He noticed that people were looking at him in a strange way—maybe even a scared way. A dog growled at him. An old lady stepped off the sidewalk to let him go by.

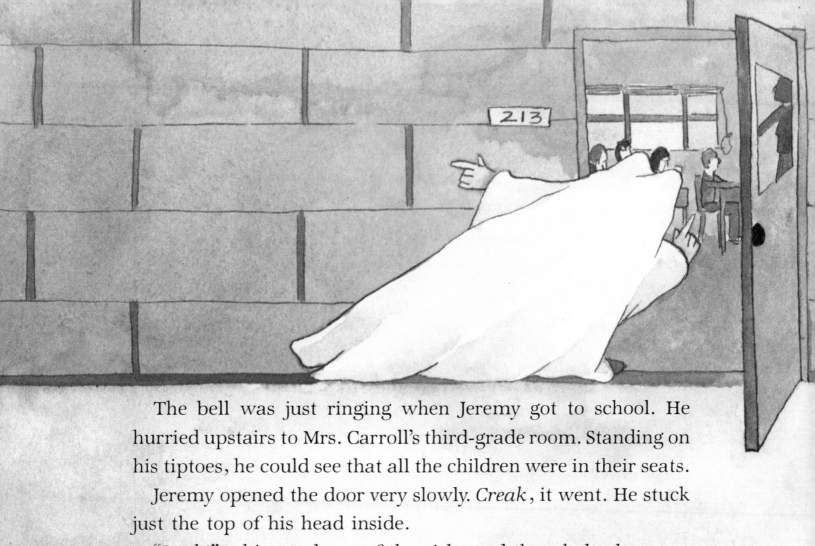

The bell was just ringing when Jeremy got to school. He hurried upstairs to Mrs. Carroll's third-grade room. Standing on his tiptoes, he could see that all the children were in their seats.

Jeremy opened the door very slowly. *Creak*, it went. He stuck just the top of his head inside.

"Look!" whispered one of the girls, and the whole class was quiet.

Jeremy poked his green nose inside, and someone screamed.
"Boo!" shouted Jeremy, jumping inside and waving his arms.
Everyone began to talk at once, and Mrs. Carroll finally had to
clap her hands for quiet. "Would you care to have a seat,
Mr. — Whoever-you-are?" she asked.

Jeremy sat down at his desk.

"Aw, it's only old Fraidy-Cat," said Marvin McGraw.

"It must be Jeremy," said Mrs. Carroll, smiling. "My, but you gave us all a fright!"

Jeremy smiled underneath his sheet. And later on, he smiled an even bigger smile. For right on the front of his sheet Mrs. Carroll pinned an orange ribbon with big black letters that said, "First Prize—Scariest."

Walking home that afternoon, Jeremy felt taller than he ever had before. He saw lots of people he knew, but they didn't know him. "Boo," he said to every tree, sometimes in a loud voice and sometimes very soft. He didn't even cross the street when he passed the haunted house.

Jeremy kept his sheet on all through dinner.

"You'll spill your beets, Jeremy," warned his father.

"I'm not Jeremy," said Jeremy. "I'm a ghost."

He ate very fast, without spilling anything, and then he and Mary Anne got their shopping bags to go trick-or-treating.

They rang all the doorbells on Walnut Street. Then they rang all the doorbells on Hemlock. It was starting to get dark, and their shopping bags were full.

"Let's go home," said Mary Anne.

At the corner they met an Indian, a princess, and a skeleton.

"How!" said the Indian, raising his tomahawk.

"Hi, Marvin," said Mary Anne. "Hi, Rosie and Nick."

"Boo," said Jeremy.

They walked up the hill to Walnut Street together. They walked past the haunted house, and Jeremy's heart only beat a little bit faster. Then Marvin stopped.

With a mean Marvin smile, he said, "Hey, Fraidy-Cat, did you ring *that* doorbell?" He pointed at the haunted house.

Jeremy's heart suddenly beat a whole lot faster. He didn't say anything.

"I dare you," said Marvin. "I double, triple dare you."

Everyone looked at Jeremy. They all knew you couldn't turn down a triple dare.

Jeremy swallowed hard. "Okay," he said finally, "I will if you will."

Everyone looked at Marvin. Marvin looked at his tomahawk.

"Fraidy-Cat," said Mary Anne.

"Who's afraid?" said Marvin. "Let's go, Jeremy."

Jeremy and Marvin tiptoed up the front walk. *Creak, creak, creak,* they tiptoed up the steps.

There they were on the porch. Nothing happened. The house was dark and quiet.

"Pssst!"

Jeremy held his breath, but it was only Mary Anne.

"We're coming, too!" she whispered. Three shadows drifted up the walk and turned into Mary Anne and Rosie and Nick.

"Look," whispered Nick. "The front door is open."

They all looked. It was true. The door was open just a crack, and a ray of light from the streetlamp shone inside.

Squeak, squeak, squeak, they tiptoed to the door. Marvin pushed it open, and Jeremy held his breath again. But except for a cricket in the grass outside, everything was quiet.

They stepped inside. The room was very dark, and it smelled like the attic at Jeremy's grandmother's house.

"There are the stairs," whispered Mary Anne, pointing somewhere.

Jeremy looked where the stairs should be. Instead of stairs he saw two huge, bright green eyes. Two huge, bright green eyes were coming toward them.

"Yeek!" cried Marvin. "It's the ghost!"

He scrambled for the door, and found it at the same time Mary Anne did. They fell in a tangle of arms and legs, knocking over their shopping bags.

The eyes came closer. They seemed to be making a strange hissing noise.

Mary Anne and Marvin got untangled and ran down the steps. Rosie and Nick were right behind them.

Only Jeremy was left, pressed against the wall by the door.

The eyes came closer and closer, and his heart beat in his ears as loud as a drum, and he wanted to run. But he didn't.

He thought about being a ghost, and about the ribbon that said, "First Prize—Scariest," and he took a deep breath.

"Boo," he said in a small voice.

The hissing sound stopped.

"Boo!" said Jeremy, louder this time.

Then he noticed that the eyes weren't so huge after all. They were close to the ground, so they couldn't belong to a very big ghost. They came closer, and then Jeremy felt something touch his leg.

He put his hand down slowly and touched the thing. It was soft and warm, and it made another sound.

"Purr," it said.

Very carefully, Jeremy picked it up and held it to the light. It was small and very thin and all black except for its eyes. Its claws dug into Jeremy's shoulder and it cried, "Meow!"

"Hey," said Jeremy in surprise. "You're the one who's scared."

He carried it outside and put it down. The kitten walked in a circle, curling itself around Jeremy's legs.

"Come on," said Jeremy, starting up the street.

'Meow," said the kitten, and Jeremy walked back and picked it up.

He held it close, all warmth and fur and ribs. And underneath his sheet he smiled a great big smile.

"Come on, Ghost," he said. "We're going home."